£5.50
UK only

Kruds beware! This book belongs to

Name Anthony   Age 10

Address 89 Markham Ave

Postcode LS8 4Jd

My favourite colour is red

My favourite Verigreen is FLYNN

My favourite Krud is Captain   (Yuck!)

Copyright © 1996 Fantome animation – Ellipse
programme – France 3 – Neurones – RTBF Imagique
– Club d'investissement Media (programme media de
l'union Europeenne)

Published in Great Britain in 1996 by World
International Limited
Deanway Technology Centre
Wilmslow Road
Handforth
Cheshire SK9 3FB

Printed in Great Britain

ISBN: 0 7498 2813 7

Written by Joyce McAleer and John Broadhead
Illustrated by Peter Wilks, Simon Girling & Associates
Designed by Viv Harper

CONTENTS

HERE COME THE...

IN the beginning there was darkness and gloom on the Black Planet of the Kruds. It was worse than a wet winter's afternoon when you have 'flu and have to stay in bed. There *was* life for the Kruds — if you can call it that. But all that cold,

misery and hard work...why, it makes even *homework* sound like fun!

If it hadn't been for the timely arrival of the strange and colourful Prism which crashed onto the surface of the planet, the place would be the same

today. Just the way the Kruds would still like it to be, in fact.

But everything changes, and the Prism brought energy, colour and happiness to this strange land. Bright, bustling, cheerful little creatures, known as Verigreens, started to flourish in the midst of the long-faced inhabitants. Beautiful flowers began to bloom among the dreary tangles of thorns which grew everywhere. And – guess what! – even the sun started to shine for once!

Nowadays the Kruds and the Verigreens live a rather uneasy existence alongside one another, separated not only by borders but by their completely different ways of life. The Kruds are ruled from the Stump headquarters by their Queen, Katheter, a tall, fearsome monarch whose main claim to fame seems to be that she is always too blinking cold! To give her credit, she's well organised, with a bossy minister-in-chief called Draffsack; a general dogsbody named Fugg; Kopious, the chief barker; and a bright (but only in the brainbox sense!) inventor chap called Sinapse. And the Kruds *look* about as attractive as they sound! Enough to put you off your beans on toast for keeps!

Now, Katheter couldn't manage without Sinapse: he invented the Hypotherm, after all – and he's the

only one who can keep it going. And, in return for his loyalty, Katheter lets him live! The Hypo, by the way, is best described as a sort of giant do-it-yourself central-heating system whose sole purpose is really to stop Katheter chilling out. As you'd expect in Krud City, it's hardly a 'green' machine, as it needs to be fed constantly with wood to keep its fire burning. That's where all the Queen's subjects come in. They spend most of their time like slaves, collecting twigs of flower wood and chucking them into the 24-hour boiler with a less-than-cheery chant of "Long live the Queen!"

The worker Kruds don't have any choice but to serve her majesty, as she runs a tight ship. Her Krud army is headed by Wasabi – a real nice guy, if you like folk with an attitude problem and snapping pincers growing out of their foreheads! Under him are the blundering Captain Drumsturdy (well-balanced by a chip on each shoulder!) and the even dafter Corporal Greeb. Oh, yes, and there are the less-than-useless Methane Brothers – two footsoldiers with at least four left feet between them!

We haven't mentioned Prince Maximillian yet, and his mum, Queen Katheter, would probably prefer us not to! He may be a Krud, but in spirit he's a true Verigreen. When cleaned up, he looks just like one!

The Kruds represent only half of the Insektors' story. In complete contrast to their jealous enemies, the Verigreens are a truly happy band. All beautifully coloured, they have a love of nature and flowers. Godfrey is the chief, a kind and thoughtful fellow who devotes himself to keeping the Prism happy with Coloured Pollen. In return, the Prism's fountain and pool of energy supply a rich and a benevolent life force which brings radiance and joy to Flower City.

Godfrey has a helpful assistant, Bentley, who helps him keep everything ticking over nicely at their base at the top of the Great Flower. Alex is Godfrey's clever scientist daughter, and her adventurous adopted brother is called Flynn. They

bicker a lot, but they're really very close.

Ever seen what looks like a flying mechanical horse, complete with saddle and a firefly perched on her tail? You soon will! That's Peg, who's not only the best means of transport ever devised to get Flynn out of scrapes but also his best friend. Oh, sorry, Elmo the firefly, *you're* his equal best friend too!

Unlike the Kruds, the Verigreens aren't into military might, though we mustn't, of course, forget the

Squadron. They're a flying fleet of exquisite dragonflies who are a real force to be reckoned with when the going gets tough.

No, the real Verigreen army is a peaceful one – a multitude of Bees! These buzzing colour harvesters are always hard at work collecting Pollen to keep the Prism in glowing health.

So that's the way the cookie crumbles in the World of Insektors. Now it's time for you to sit back and read more of their exciting adventures. And remember – think *small*!

Alex's Word Garden

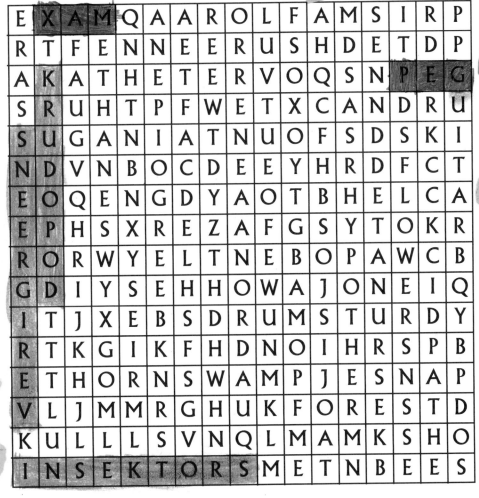

E	X	A	M	Q	A	A	R	O	L	F	A	M	S	I	R	P
R	T	F	E	N	N	E	E	R	U	S	H	D	E	T	D	P
A	K	A	T	H	E	T	E	R	V	O	Q	S	N	P	E	G
S	R	U	H	T	P	F	W	E	T	X	C	A	N	D	R	U
S	U	G	A	N	I	A	T	N	U	O	F	S	D	S	K	I
N	D	V	N	B	O	C	D	E	E	Y	H	R	D	F	C	T
E	O	Q	E	N	G	D	Y	A	O	T	B	H	E	L	C	A
E	P	H	S	X	R	E	Z	A	F	G	S	Y	T	O	K	R
R	O	R	W	Y	E	L	T	N	E	B	O	P	A	W	C	B
G	D	I	Y	S	E	H	H	O	W	A	J	O	N	E	I	Q
I	T	J	X	E	B	S	D	R	U	M	S	T	U	R	D	Y
R	T	K	G	I	K	F	H	D	N	O	I	H	R	S	P	B
E	T	H	O	R	N	S	W	A	M	P	J	E	S	N	A	P
V	L	J	M	M	R	G	H	U	K	F	O	R	E	S	T	D
K	U	L	L	L	S	V	N	Q	L	M	A	M	K	S	H	O
I	N	S	E	K	T	O	R	S	M	E	T	N	B	E	E	S

Alex has planted the twenty words shown below in her flowerbed – and your job is to find them all! You'll need to look carefully, though, as they may run backwards, forwards, up or down. Answers on Page 61.

~~INSEKTORS~~	PRISMAFLORA	KATHETER	BENTLEY
~~VERIGREENS~~	FOUNTAIN	DRUMSTURDY	ELMO
~~KRUD-O-POD~~	THORNSWAMP	~~MAX~~	~~PEG~~
HYPOTHERM	FLOWERS	GREEB	SQUADRON
GUITAR	FOREST	METHANES	BEES

THE PRISM

If it weren't for **The Prism** there would be no Verigreens – nor even any colours to brighten up the world of the Kruds! This mysterious meteor had been whizzing through space since the beginning of creation before it crash-landed on the Dark Planet. With all that time to chew things over, you'd think it would have picked somewhere less gloomy for its new home.

Never mind, it brought its wonderful energy and 'lighten up a little' message to the place, and, in gratitude, it is tended with loving care by Godfrey and his friends in Flower City!

12

The Guardian of The Prism is a master botanist – that's someone good with flowers, to you and me! Who better, then, than **Godfrey**! A grand and majestic butterfly he may be, but when he talks he sounds more like a nutty old professor. He's a good sort, though – friendly, helpful and he always looks on the bright side. Godfrey is Alex and Flynn's dad, and he plays a mean tune on The Colour Organ, which feeds the vital Energy Fountain of The Prism.

13

ALEX

Wow – even as butterflies go, there's no-one more lovely in the whole of Flower City than Godfrey's charming daughter **Alex**! She's very capable and kind, though she never stops arguing with her adopted brother Flynn. Tougher than she looks, she's always eager to stand at the front line when it comes to protecting her fellow Verigreens from the endless invasions of the crafty Kruds. Alex has got it all: she combines beauty with brains, for she's also a brill scientist who specialises in fighting disease and creating longer-lasting flowers. In short, though Alex is a butterfly, you could say she's even busier than a bee!

FLYNN

A brave buccaneer… a modern-day Robin Hood …a mint musician? **Flynn** will tell you he's all of these – but *we're* not completely convinced! Seriously though, Flynn is quite a guy, and a bit of a hero in Flower City. He laughs in the face of danger – and that's probably why he usually finds himself up to his neck in it! Flynn is the adopted son of Godfrey. His parents are unknown, but are thought to be Kruds who saw the light! He's normally to be found strumming away on his Colour Guitar, a special weapon with the amazing power to turn crusty Kruds into Verigreens. Don't tell anyone, but the truth is he just *loves* playing it!

15

BENTLEY

Look down to earth and you won't find anyone more down-to-earth than good old **Bentley**, Godfrey's chief assistant and right-hand – er – man! This loyal and dedicated Steward of the Federation of Pollen Gatherers – to give him his full title – plays a vital role in Flower City. Well, *he* reckons he does, anyway! And if by any chance he ever puts a spanner in the works and loses his job, he could always work on TV.

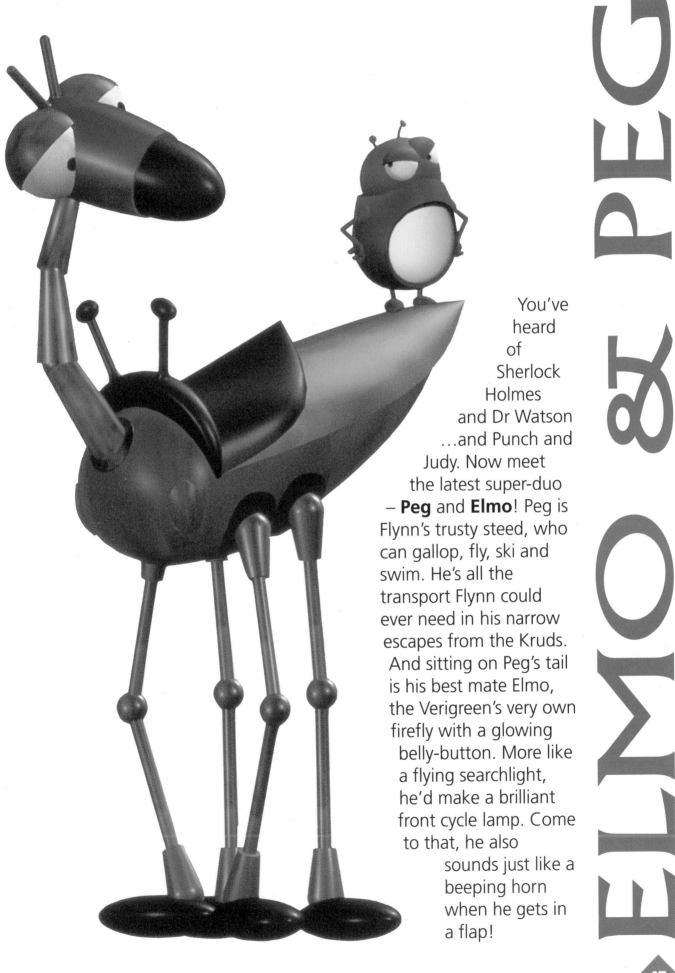

ELMO & PEG

You've heard of Sherlock Holmes and Dr Watson …and Punch and Judy. Now meet the latest super-duo – **Peg** and **Elmo**! Peg is Flynn's trusty steed, who can gallop, fly, ski and swim. He's all the transport Flynn could ever need in his narrow escapes from the Kruds. And sitting on Peg's tail is his best mate Elmo, the Verigreen's very own firefly with a glowing belly-button. More like a flying searchlight, he'd make a brilliant front cycle lamp. Come to that, he also sounds just like a beeping horn when he gets in a flap!

THE colour guitar

"I *love* this job!" declared Bentley, sitting back and resting his feet on the Colour Organ. "I've worked here ever since I was a maggot. I remember when a Verigreen could collect Pollen from afar without fear of being attacked by the Kruds."

"Yes, those were the days," mumbled Godfrey absent-mindedly, as he fiddled about with a peculiar-looking stringed instrument on the table. "A-ha, finished at last!"

Smiling triumphantly, he lifted up the device, placed it carefully in Alex's hands and asked her to take it to Flynn.

"What is it?" she asked.

"Well, it *was* his old guitar," explained Godfrey. "But now it's a musical gun that shoots colours whenever he plays!"

"Hee! That'll knock the clogs off the Kruds," chuckled Bentley. "Hit them, and they'll turn *veri-green* indeed!"

In the Flower Forest, Flynn was overjoyed when Alex delivered his

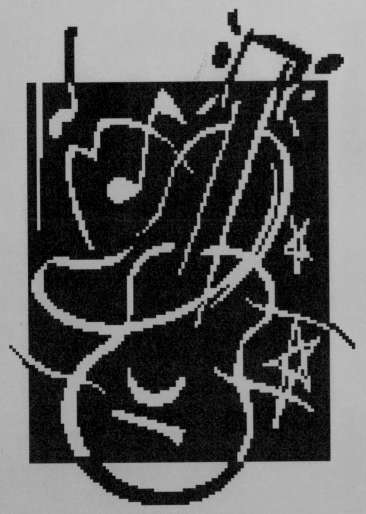

new Colour Guitar. He decided to get in some practice immediately so that he could perform later at the Colour Communion.

"The old feller's done a great job!" he grinned, beginning to strum a pleasant summery melody. "Wow, look at that!"

As he played, beautiful big exploding blobs of bright colours burst from the Guitar and shot high into the air! Alex watched in amazement – and so did Fugg and his Krud pals Oozy and Runny, who were spying on them from some nearby undergrowth.

"*There's* trouble for you!" murmured Fugg. Then his voice turned to a whine as the cascading colours sprinkled over his two comrades. "Aargh! Fall-out!"

But it was too late: Oozy and Runny instantly turned colourful and began grinning and giggling foolishly.

"Bah, I *hate* those Verigreens," growled Fugg. "They make my shell itch!"

Back at Krud City, Sinapse and Draffsack were, as usual, fighting a losing battle to keep the boiler running. When *it* was warm, the *Queen* was happy... well, less miserable, anyway!

"Fugg the fatuous returning in failure!" announced Kopious impudently.

An excited Fugg scurried into the Hypotherm to bring Draffsack news of the Colour Guitar. "And look what happens, boyo!" he exclaimed, pointing to the now multi-coloured Oozy and Runny, who were amiably discussing their favourite shades of purple.

"Put them in the Krud-o-Pod!" ordered Draffsack.

The gibbering pair were placed at one end of a giant machine which resembled an elephant's medieval family-size dishwasher. After several minutes of grinding and sucking and much whirring of cogwheels, Oozy and Runny emerged, both dark and nasty again, from the other side of the Krud-o-Pod.

"Now get them out of my sight," sighed Draffsack. He turned his attention to the awesome Wasabi. "As commander-in-chief of the Black Guard, the honour of securing this new threat to the Krud nation falls upon you. Don't blow it!"

Wasabi stood even more sharply to attention and clicked his pincers obediently.

Deep in the Flower Forest, Fugg's hand crept out slyly and grabbed Flynn's Guitar. He made his escape, but stumbled noisily.

"What's that!?" cried Flynn. "A Krud! Elmo, give us some light!"

Jumping onto Peg, and with Elmo flying ahead on full-beam, Flynn went in hot pursuit of Fugg and the Guitar. But the wily Wasabi was waiting in ambush.

He pulled back a trailing tree-branch and thwacked Flynn off Peg and into a smelly swamp.

"Oh, dear, I look like a Krud now," groaned Flynn, covered from head to toe in thick mud. Then his eyes brightened. "And that's given me a brilliant idea!"

Presently the now murky brown and Krud-like Flynn and Elmo joined a line of Kruds carrying bundles of flower wood to the ever-hungry Hypotherm.

"Hear that?" whispered Flynn, hearing

a familiar twanging in the distance. "It's my Guitar! Let's get it!"

In his laboratory, Sinapse was examining the Colour Guitar. "I think," he mused, "we could cross-phase the K-waves from this guitar and – "

"Shut it," came back Draffsack. "I want that thing destroyed!"

Suddenly a bundle of twigs socked Sinapse on the head and sent him flying. Flynn and Elmo had arrived!

"Guards! Guards!" screamed Draffsack. Flynn snatched his Guitar and fired it.

A coloured beam hit Draffsack, and turned him silly. Flynn mounted a

Krudmobile and shot away, with Elmo as his guiding-light.

They were soon spotted. Captain Drumsturdy and Corporal Greeb jumped onto another Krudmobile and raced after them. More Kruds quickly followed and soon there was a thrilling chase through the maze of gloomy castle corridors as Flynn zoomed around to find his way to freedom!

Finally, Flynn and Elmo burst through the castle doors and soared high into the air.

"Quite nippy the Mark III Krudmobile, isn't it!?" observed one dozy Methane gatekeeper to his

brother.

"I think I'm out of fuel!" cried Flynn to Elmo, as the Krudmobile's motor spluttered and coughed. But Peg, loyal as ever, was hovering nearby and waiting to come to the rescue! Flynn grasped his Guitar firmly and made a daring mid-air jump onto his back. "Take us home, Peg, or we'll miss showtime!"

Everyone in Flower City was waiting for the Colour Communion to begin, but it couldn't start without Flynn and his Guitar.

"Where on earth is the lad?" tutted Godfrey impatiently.

"Probably still in bed," scoffed Alex.

"Call this a concert? I've had more fun at the Jobcentre," grumbled Bentley.

But then the music started! Beautiful, bright music accompanied by explosions of brilliant colours shooting high into the heavens like a grand fireworks display. All the Verigreens looked up and gasped with delight. It was Flynn standing on a flower high above and playing as he had never done before.

"That's my boy!" beamed Godfrey proudly. But no one could hear him over the tremendous cheering that came from the assembled Verigreens as they began to dance around to the Flynn beat!

GRAB that Guitar!

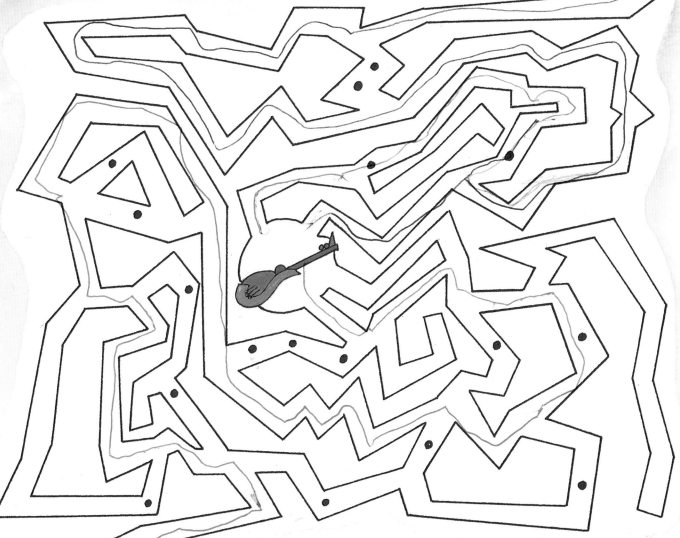

Your mission, should you not decide to tidy your room instead, is to join Flynn on a 'borrowed' Krudmobile and snatch back the Colour Guitar! Enter Krud City, grab the Guitar and get out again *pronto*. But each time you pass a dreaded Black Spot, you lose precious fuel. Pick up six spots and you're *grounded* on the spot – and at the mercy of shivering Queen Katheter! The trick is to escape with as few spots as possible. Less than four means you're a real chump – sorry, *champ*! *(Answer on Page 61)*

The BIG Krudword

Across

3. Daffodils, in short!
6. He announces the arrival of Kruds
7. Verries like to breathe this in when it's fresh!
8. Leaves turn – – – – – in summer
10. Keeper of the Prism
11. The dragonfly fighting force
13. Commander of the Krud army
15. The Verries live in Flower – – – –
17. Max *loves* her!
18. Elmo's companion
19. Everything grows in the Flower – – – – – –!
22. The name for brightly coloured Insektors
24. The Guitar man
25. Insects you wouldn't want in your pants!
26. What this Annual is all about…

Down

1. Mix red and yellow to get this colour
2. The coldest season of the year
3. Katheter's chief minister
4. Look out for – – – –buckets!
5. Where you'll find all the colours in the sky
6. The Krud version of a motorbike!
7. Katheter would love to sit in front of a – – – – – – – fire!
12. A short snooze
14. Prince of Kruds
16. The top Krud!
18. Bees collect this
20. You use it to build a castle on the beach
21. What's left after wood is burned
23. Flower that's a girl's name!

24

INSEKTORS ART GALLERY

AMAZE *your pals by sketching your own picture of Flynn and his arch-enemy Wasabi. It's easy! Just draw out faint pencil squares on a big sheet of paper, then copy these illustrations carefully, square by square. Colour in your pics and you've cracked it. (If you've only got a black pen, better start with miserable old Wasabi!)*

The Escape

MAX was looking through his periscope at the land of the Verigreens when he was interrupted by Queen Katheter and Draffsack.

"That's no way for a Krud to carry on," whined Draffsack.

"Shut up, you noxious little creep," snapped the Queen. "It's your job to turn this weakling into a Prince worthy of the name Krud!"

Draffsack pushed Max into his room and slammed the door. The young Prince pulled back his rug to reveal a hole – his latest escape venture! He climbed down and began tunnelling. It wasn't long before he burst through a connecting wall and found himself, unexpectedly, in the Stump's service bay, where Corporal Greeb was repairing a Frogbucket – a huge mechanical transport machine.

Max poked idly at the machine's control levers and knobs. "What's this button do, Greeb?"

"Don't touch that, your Highness...Oh, no!"

The Frogbucket lurched into life! Greeb fell backwards and Max took the opportunity to jump into the driver's seat. Hearing Greeb's cry, Draffsack and Drumsturdy raced in, just in time to see the Frogbucket stomping away.

"What's wrong!?" demanded Draffsack.

"The Prince has gone off with me sandwiches!" warbled Greeb. "Egg and cress, they were, too."

Now in Verigreen territory, Max ejected from the cockpit and landed with a thud in the middle of a blaze of pollen-rich flowers.

"Wow – I've turned gold and yellow and purple!" he cried in excitement, scampering off into the Forest. But Draffsack and Drumsturdy were hot on his heels. They hovered on

their Krudmobile by the giant frog.

"A-ha!" said Draffsack. "Where there's an abandoned Frogbucket, what will you find nearby?"

Drumsturdy thought hard for a moment. "Greeb's sandwiches?"

"A Prince, you hare-brained haggis! Now, come on..."

Not too far away, Max was about to meet his first Verigreen. It was Alex, and she was collecting Pollen in a flask.

"Aralins for a shiny shell...hibiscus for healthy antennae...woody nightshade for Father's dandruff," she murmured.

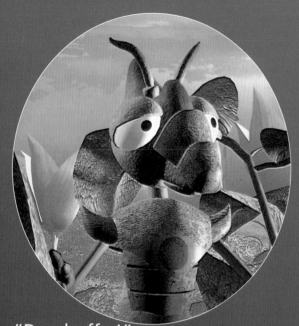

"Dandruff...!" breathed Max in admiration. He was bewitched by her gentleness and beauty.

Alex looked up. "Can I help you? Have we met before?"

"It's unlikely," mumbled Max shyly. "You see, I – er – "

The unmistakable sound of a Krudmobile approached. Alex pulled Max out of sight until Draffsack and Drumsturdy had blundered past, breaking the flask of Pollen.

"I hate Kruds!" said Alex, returning with Max to the flask. "Look – a whole morning's work wasted!"

"Does it matter?"

"Of course. Pollen helps us to live and create new flowers!"

"That's amazing!" gasped Max. "Can you make them any colour you want?"

"Sure. I'll show you. Come on." Alex flew into the air, expecting Max to follow.

"I don't know how to fly," he confessed shamefully. "And there's something you should know about me – "

"Shh...concentrate. Stick out your wings and flap."

Max followed her example and managed to flutter about a little. "You're getting there!" smiled his new friend. "My name's Alex, by the way. What's yours?"

"Max!" laughed the young Krud, who had just fallen in love with a Verigreen. "It's Max!"

Flying lessons continued. Max tried to copy Alex's loop-the-loop but he simply plummeted to the ground and sploshed into a puddle. Alex's happy face changed when he emerged from the water, for all his glorious colours had washed off. "A Krud!" she cried. "How could you *pretend* like that!"

"Alex, I was trying to tell you but –"

Whoosh! A colour beam hit Max and made him bright once again. Flynn had arrived on the scene with his Guitar, and Max ran off in fright.

"Get away and leave her alone!" yelled Flynn defensively.

"No, we must find him," implored Alex.

"Why? He's a Krud."

"Yes," replied Alex. "But a different *kind* of Krud..."

Max was sitting alone on a flower in the Forest when he was hit by another beam, but this time from a *Krud* weapon.

"Direct hit!" shouted Drumsturdy. Then his mouth gaped open. "Och, it's *you*, your Highness..."

Draffsack confronted Max angrily. "Where have you been? Your mother's furious – and it's me that gets it in the neck!"

But Max wasn't ready to be frogmarched back to Krud City.

Instead, he hopped it to freedom! He ran and ran, but he was no match for Draffsack and Drumsturdy on the Krudmobile. They were gaining on him fast and were about to capture him when a bright beam shot out of the undergrowth

and transformed Drumsturdy into a giggling heap. Flynn and his Guitar had come to the rescue!

By the waterfall, Max had his first bath. Alex helped him scrape off the black layer of soot that had made him so drab. Then she and Flynn took him to the Great Flower.

"Verigreens and Kruds are the same really," explained Godfrey. "What matters is what is in your heart, young fellow."

"You mean he can *stay* with us?" asked Alex, thrilled. Max beamed

when Godfrey nodded his head and welcomed him to Flower City.

Then is was straight outside again for more flying lessons. This time Flynn came to help too.

"Perhaps I should stay low," suggested Max nervously.

"Trust us," said Flynn.

"Just flap your wings," said Alex.

Max took off and climbed higher, but then began to fall. Alex and Flynn were there to catch him.

"Just *flap*!" said Alex encouragingly.

He did – and it worked. Max soared confidently into the air just like a Verigreen.

"I'm really *doing* it!" he yelled. "I can fly! I can actually fly!"

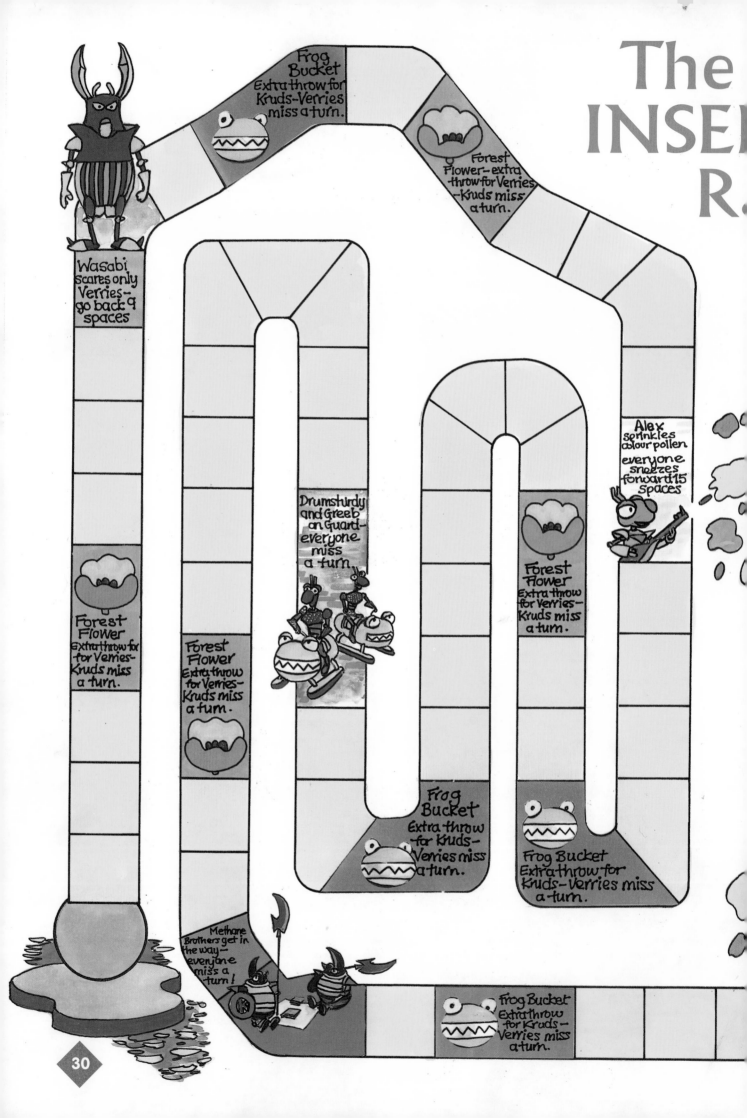

The
INSE[...]
R[...]

Frog Bucket Extra throw for Kruds-Verries miss a turn.

Forest Flower- extra throw for Verries -Kruds miss a turn.

Wasabi scares only Verries- go back 9 spaces

Alex sprinkles colour pollen everyone sneezes forward 15 spaces

Drumsturdy and Greeb on Guard- everyone miss a turn

Forest Flower Extra throw for Verries- Kruds miss a turn.

Forest Flower Extra throw for Verries- Kruds miss a turn.

Forest Flower Extra throw for Verries- Kruds miss a turn.

Frog Bucket Extra throw for Kruds- Verries miss a turn.

Frog Bucket Extra throw for Kruds- Verries miss a turn.

Methane Brothers get in the way- everyone miss a turn!

Frog Bucket Extra throw for Kruds- Verries miss a turn.

30

Great
TORS
e!

Katheter in bad mood — sends everyone the long way round! Whether you're Krud or Verigreen.

Forest Flower Extra throw for Verries — Kruds miss a turn.

Forest Flower. Extra throw for Verries — Kruds miss a turn.

Bentley doing track repairs — Verigreen and Krud go back 10 spaces

Frog Bucket Extra throw for kruds — Verries miss a turn.

Frog Bucket Extra throw for kruds — Verries miss a turn.

Flynn fires colour gun Kruds go back 9 spaces

Frog Bucket Extra throw for kruds — Verries miss a turn.

Forest Flower Extra throw for Verries — Kruds miss a turn.

To celebrate the New Year, Queen Katheter has agreed to a Great Race between Kruds and Verigreens. Got a couple of counters and a dice? Then you can join in with a friend! Decide whether you're a Verigreen or a Krud and follow the route. Throw a six and you get another throw. Whenever you land on a picture square, just obey the instructions. Good luck!

Queen Katheter

Definitely *not* the sort of person you'd allow to look after your hamster and goldfish when you go on holiday! **Queen Katheter** is proud, heartless, unscrupulous, cruel, bad-tempered… and that's on one of her *good* days! Always one degree under (Celsius, of course!), she forces the common-or-garden Kruds – who have already mined out their own fuel supply – to steal the Verigreens' flower wood. Hers is a kingdom of selfishness and greed …of taking, not giving …of darkness, not light. Got the picture? Well, don't bother sending *me* a copy!

Prince Maximillian

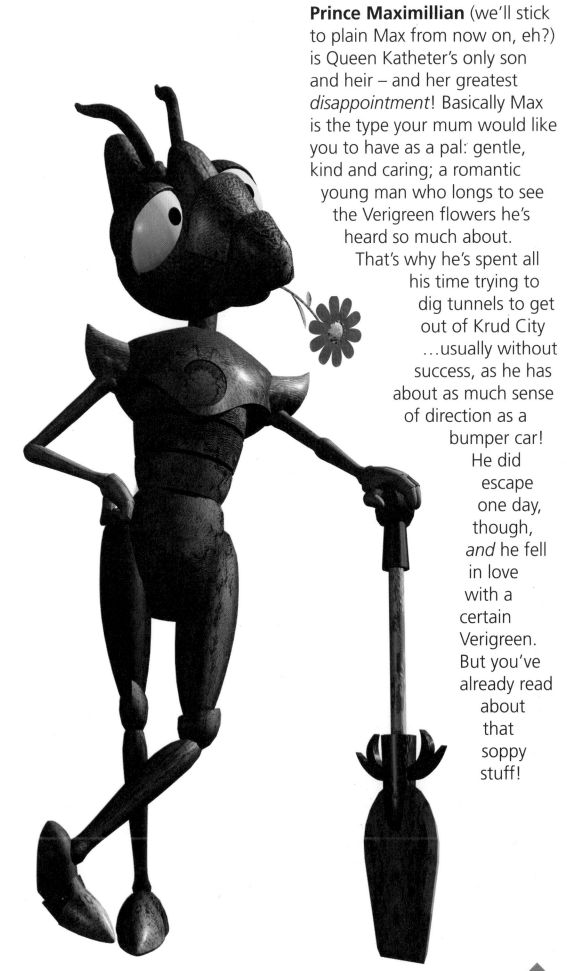

Prince Maximillian (we'll stick to plain Max from now on, eh?) is Queen Katheter's only son and heir – and her greatest *disappointment*! Basically Max is the type your mum would like you to have as a pal: gentle, kind and caring; a romantic young man who longs to see the Verigreen flowers he's heard so much about.

That's why he's spent all his time trying to dig tunnels to get out of Krud City …usually without success, as he has about as much sense of direction as a bumper car! He did escape one day, though, *and* he fell in love with a certain Verigreen. But you've already read about that soppy stuff!

33

Draffsack & Kopious

The Queen's slavish little chief-of-everything, **Draffsack** is bossy, grumpy and never, ever looks on the bright side. Any good points? Well …his bony finger, perhaps; he's good at pointing *that*!

If chief barker **Kopious** ever announces your arrival at the Court of Queen Katheter, you'll certainly know about it! He says *whatever* he likes, about whoever he likes – and it's always insulting. This pompous old stick is a real stickler for tradition, and he knows full well that, because of his position, he can get away with anything!

An omni-talented practitioner of electro-mechanical invention and innovation by royal appointment. That's how the evil genius **Sinapse** would probably describe himself in his confusing gobbledegook style! He dreams up war machines like nobody's business… but if he invites you to be a test-pilot, remember to engage brain before saying yes!

Sinapse & Fugg

More of a gopher than an Insektor, because you can always count on him to go for this and go for that! Busy little **Fugg** could be said to do the work of two men – Laurel and Hardy. And, he can sing like a dream. Whoops, sorry, that should read nightmare!

Wasabi & The Methane Brothers

If first prize in a competition were a night at the opera with **Wasabi**, second prize would be two nights! This thoroughly nasty armour-plated tank-on-legs hasn't a friendly bone in his body – more like a chassis of steel girders. What can you say about a big bully who models himself on a Samurai warrior? Answer: anything you like, 'cos he'll tread on you anyway!

The **Methane Brothers** are a real gas! Ask them to stand guard at your front door, and they'd probably let the letterbox get stolen! This pair think that multi-media means having two newspapers at the same time, and that software is what you put on when you change out of your boots! They once threw away their A to Z of Krud City because they only wanted to get from A to B!

Captain Drumsturdy & Corporal Greeb

The roaring **Captain Drumsturdy** thinks he's Rob Roy and Robbie Burns rolled into one.

As for his sidekick, **Corporal Greeb**, one kick in the side and he's out for the count. The only way he'd be any good at taking orders on manoeuvres is on a pizza delivery motorbike!

Frogbucket

The dismal Thorn Swamp is hardly the first place you'd choose for a day out – in fact, it's probably the last! But Flynn and Bentley were there for a purpose.

"And there she is – Prismaflora!" cried Bentley. "She only blooms once a year, y'know."

The two Verigreens crept forward cautiously to where the beautiful, rare bloom was nestling amid a tangle of sharp thorns.

"Ee, she's right gradely," said Bentley. "The only flower that will bring life back to the Prism. I'll take the Pollen and we'll be off…"

"Hurry up, Bentley. We're not safe here," urged Flynn. He glanced nervously from side to side and then checked his back. "Aaaargh!"

Right behind him stood a Frogbucket complete with staring, bulging eyes and a greedy, snapping mouth the size of a removal van.

"Aaargh!" yelled Bentley, like an echo.

"Take that!" cried Flynn, recovering his senses and bombarding the creature with all the colours he could get out of his Guitar.

But his efforts had no effect; the

great frog was immune to his weapon. It stomped forward, opened its mouth and prepared to devour the two Verries. Then Flynn had a brainwave: he jumped sideways, waved and invited the frog to follow him.

"This way, there's a good boy!" he teased, leading his clanking enemy nearer and nearer to a convenient swamp.

Splat! The frog lurched to the edge of the muddy waters, lost its balance and fell in with a juicy squelching noise. One of its eyes opened and Captain Drumsturdy appeared. He'd been steering the clumsy amphibian!

"Ye winged beasties won't escape ma Frogbucket next time!" he screamed, grabbing angrily at his control levers. "Lucky for you I'm away home now for ma cheese toasties!"

In the Great Flower, Flynn breathlessly told Godfrey the bad news about the Frogbucket and what had happened in the Thorn Swamp.

"I were useless," confessed Bentley. "I'm feeling right under the weather."

"A quick swim in the Energy Pool and you'll be fine," said Alex.

Godfrey gave her a worried look and pointed to the sad Prism. "I'm afraid it's not that simple, my dear. Without some Prismaflora Pollen, the source of all our energy will die..."

"At least we know where it's flowering," said Flynn. Then, with a determined expression, he added: "I'm going out now...to fix a frog!"

What Flynn didn't know was that the Kruds had a whole army of Frogbuckets, the fiendish invention of the misguided but clever Sinapse. At that precise moment Draffsack and Sinapse were insecting – sorry, *inspecting* – a line of the mechanical monsters at the Stump.

"Never seen fitter-looking frogs! They'll strike terror into those flowery creeps!" cackled Draffsack. "Now we can tear down the Flower Forest and have plenty of wood to relight the Hypotherm!"

Far above, Peg dived down from the clouds and dropped off Flynn and Elmo in their renewed search for the elusive Prismaflora.

"If you see anything the size of a tower block that hops, let me know!" joked Flynn.

Scarcely had he spoken than they spotted the massed ranks of Frogbuckets.

"Wow!" cried Flynn. "He's brought all his friends this time! Better get away from, here – finding the Prismaflora is our priority right now!"

"Forward, ma bonny laddies... a-hunting we will go!" came Drumsturdy's loud command from inside the leading Frogbucket, and, with that, the army of wood gobblers began to invade the precious Flower Forest.

It didn't take Flynn, Elmo and Peg long to locate the Prismaflora again.

"Beautiful! We've caught it in full bloom," declared Flynn. "With all this Colour Pollen the Prism will soon recover and Bentley will be his old self again! What could go wrong!?"

Plenty – a giant Frogbucket marched up smartly from behind and gobbled up Flynn and Elmo!

Alex was wandering aimlessly through the Forest when Peg ran up, honking madly at her.

"Flynn? Eaten!?" she exclaimed in disbelief. "And the Frogbuckets are trampling all the flowers? This is *definitely* a job for the Squadron!"

Within minutes the Dragonflies had scrambled for action and were already airborne. They dived low and fast, hitting the marching Frogbuckets with bombs of Coloured Pollen. But the robotic creatures were not affected in the least, and they trundled on relentlessly.

Flynn and Elmo were still inside one of the Frogbuckets and being thrown from side to side. Flynn discovered a hatch leading to the frogeye cockpit. Climbing up, he found himself behind Corporal

Greeb in the driver's seat. He took out a colour bomb, placed it under Greeb's seat and waited for the inevitable explosion. *Bam!*

"Oh, I *love* surprises!" giggled Greeb, changing colour rapidly. "I think it's time for a tango!"

He then began jerking crazily at his levers and sent the Frogbucket into a frenetic dancing routine.

Alex, nearby, was relieved to see Flynn and Elmo make their escape. But she was astonished to see the two Verries, with Peg's help, fly back inside *another* Frogbucket, and out again. Then in and out of another...and another... and another...

"You're out of your minds!" yelled Alex. "What are you doing!?"

It soon became obvious. Flynn had been planting a colour bomb under each driver's seat – and now he was getting results! One by one, each Frogbucket exploded in a haze

of brilliant colours, then stopped marching and started dancing!

"Get a grip on yourselves, laddies!" yelled Drumsturdy in vain, as the air filled with the infectious giggling of all his fellow Frogbucket pilots. But it was all over: the Captain had lost yet another battle!

Flynn, Alex and Bentley watched anxiously as Godfrey poured the vital Prismaflora Pollen into the Prism's Energy Pool.

"Hope we have enough," murmured Flynn, crossing his fingers. "Don't fancy going back for more..."

The Pool began to shimmer and glimmer a little, then a bit more and a bit more until – whoosh! – the Energy shot up the Fountain.

"Eh up...by heck!" cried Bentley, jumping into the Pool. He laughed with glee as his fading colours were instantly restored to their former brilliance by the healing powers of the waters. "Me and the Prism...we're saved! I'm feeling better already!"

What sort of petrol do you put in a Volkswagen Beetle?
Shell!

Why don't Verries like lawnmowers?
They have a lot of bovver with a hover!

What do you call an Insektor from France?
A cross-channel Verrie!

Which Verigreen travels even faster than a Krudmobile?
A Bentley Turbo!

Which shop sells only vegetables?
A veri-greengrocers!

Godfrey: What do you get if you add 653, 254 and 963?
Bentley: A headache!

What are the Prism's favourite letters?
N...R...G (en-er-gy!)

Where do tadpoles borrow money from?
A frog's pawn broker!

What happened when the two Kruds threw red and blue Pollen at one another?
A violet struggle took place!

Who brings presents for Krud kids at Christmas?
Santa claws!

Laugh with the Verigreens

What is Alex's favourite book?
Wuthering Flights!

Where's the best place to sleep if you get locked out?
In a flower-bed!

What's the cure for a nasty sting?
Anti-bee-otics!

Who is Flynn's favourite detective?
Insektor Morse!

Alex: Got a flower petal?
Flynn: Sorry, no – and don't call me petal!

What is the Verigreens favourite TV programme?
Prismer Cell Block H!

Max: Is this Pollen going to Blackfriars?
Alex: No, it's going to Turnham Green!

What flies round flowers and moans?
A grumble-bee!

How do spiders keep in touch?
On the internet web!

A FROGBUCKET CAKE

It's easy to make a Frogbucket cake for your next party! Ask a grown-up to cut two sponge cake shapes for the head and body (they don't need to be very accurate). Put one on top of the other and cover with green icing. For the froggy eyes, add two round mints and Smarties, then finish off by piping a zig-zag mouth. Enjoy!

THE WRIGGLER!

Draw a spiral on a large sheet of paper and colour it to make a curly snake (with its head in the centre). Ask a parent to cut it out and hang it by cotton over a radiator (not a fire or cooker). The warm currents of rising air will make your Wriggler twist and turn endlessly!

COLOURS OF THE RAINBOW

Red, orange, yellow, green, blue, indigo and violet... here's a clever way to remember all the colours of the rainbow in order. Just make up your own memorable sentence using the initial letters – like *Richard of York goes bananas in Vancouver*!

YOUR OWN FLOWER GARDEN

Fancy a Flower Garden in your bedroom? Place a sheet of blotting paper in a shallow tray, scatter on mustard or cress seeds, then add carrot-tops (ask a parent to cut them). Stand it in a sunny place and water daily ...you'll soon have a lovely lawn and bushes! In the meantime, you can make little Kruds and Verries for your garden. Use coloured modelling clay for heads and bodies, and pipe cleaners for arms and antennae!

CATCH A KRUD!

Take a small piece of thick card and get a parent to thread a big loop of thin, strong string through it as shown.

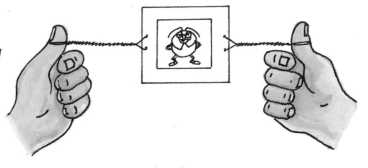

On one side of the card, draw a Krud; on the other side, a box. Wind up the string, hold it between your thumbs and pull. When the card spins, your Krud will appear to be caught in the box!

45

VERIGREEN FAMILY TREE

Can you recognise all your
Verigreen pals from their
silhouettes?
(Answers on Page 61)

1

2

3

4

5

6
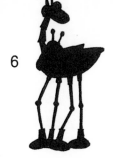

7

KRUD FAMILY TANGLE

Now it's time to spot the
Kruds – even if you
wouldn't like to meet
them on a dark night!
(Answers on Page 61)

1

2

3

4

5

6

7

8

9

10

46

Sinapse's potty inventions
THE ONES THAT GOT AWAY!

PEDAL-POWER TELEVISION

This brilliant exercise bike was supposed to raise Queen Katheter's temperature as she pedalled away and watched TV. But – you guessed it – she made *me* do all the hard work while she sat back and enjoyed her favourite soaps. I was hoping to get a medal, but all I got was a bad back instead!

INFRA-RED VERRIE DETECTOR

General Wasabi was going through a bad patch recently, so to cheer him up, I designed this advanced triple-diode device to help him spot a Verrie at a thousand paces. Trouble is, it also picks up heavy metal stations – and once Wasabi gets that rhythm in his head, there's just no stopping him!

THE WOODMOBILE

My dream was to build the Mark IV Krudmobile out of flower wood. No rust or metal fatigue, you see! Great idea, eh? No way – the first prototype caught fire, the second one caught a nasty case of woodworm, and the third just wooden go!

The mechanical digger

Simple ideas are often the best ones, so they say. That's not usually the way Sinapse works, though: most of his inventions usually go the long way round to do something you could do better *yourself*! One day, however, he had a blinding flash of inspiration. It happened when one of Max's escape tunnels collapsed and a Methane Brother fell on the young Prince's head.

"Eureka!" cried Sinapse gleefully. "Roots and capillaries are the answer!"

"Explain yourself," sighed Draffsack wearily.

"It's all very simple," burbled the inventor. "When we attack The Verries on the ground, we get – "

"Hammered?"

"Exactly! So we need to go *underground* in a tunnel. To use words of one syllable, we use a clinker-built, lamelliform stratified exfoliator. That's a Digger to you!"

A week or so later, Alex was doing a spot of gardening. Flynn was there, too, but he wasn't much help.

"This new tulip's lovely," he teased. "We'll call it Alex – because it's tall and skinny and has a big head, just like my little

sister!"

"Shut up, Flynn," came her reply. "And I'm not your little sister. Sometimes you're such a pain..."

Their argument would have become more heated if it hadn't been for a loud rumbling from below. The ground began to tremble, and one by one, Alex's carefully tended tulips began to disappear

straight down into the soil.

"What is it!?" asked Alex, alarmed.

"I think we have a serious mole problem." Her brother smiled weakly, but he looked worried. He might have said more, had *he* not then suddenly disappeared downwards like the flowers!

Flynn found himself in a wide underground tunnel. His eyes took a few seconds to get used to the darkness before he realised he was face to face with the 'mole' – a huge boring-machine! Even more boring, Wasabi was on guard down there.

"No let escape!" was Wasabi's pleasant greeting. "Give up!"

"Flynn...up here!" came Alex's voice from above.

No contest! Flynn took the better offer and fluttered upwards. Alex helped him struggle out of the hole.

"Do I get a thank you, *little*

brother?" she asked.

"*Big* brother, if you don't mind," he replied shakily. Then, under his breath, he muttered: "And thank you!"

"I don't like the sound of this at all," declared Godfrey, shaking his head as Flynn briefed him about the trouble down below.

"Flynn says the machine had a big round thing with four letters on it," added Alex.

"I think you're describing a compass...and that's bad news for *us*," said Godfrey. "It means the Kruds can navigate underground with extreme accuracy!"

At that precise moment the Kruds were talking compasses too. In the Stump, Sinapse was showing off to Queen Katheter and Draffsack.

"My plan is so daring and so cunningly simple, it nearly makes me sick," he gushed. "The compass will guide my Mechanical Digger right to the roots of Flower City. We'll pull it into the earth and bury it forever...and then we'll have all the flower wood we ever need!"

"Ha, the Verigreens will be lying low – *veri-low* indeed!" joked Katheter. Not much of a joke, but it was about as funny as she ever got!
"Hee, the Royal wit's as sharp as ever," whined Draffsack.

"Don't overdo it, Draffsack," retorted Katheter. "Fail and you die."

She left with the suspicion of a smile on her lips, thinking of how delightful life would be without colour...without flowers...without Verigreens!

More and more tulips were doing a disappearing act, and Godfrey was preparing a counter-attack. He showed a powerful magnet to Alex, Flynn and Elmo.

"This is *our* secret weapon," he announced. "If we can place this under the control panel of the Kruds' mechanical digger, their compass will go – "

"Bananas!" grinned Flynn.

The ground started to shudder as the Mechanical Digger approached Flower City. The time had come for action. Flynn and Elmo raced to the Tulip Field.

"Hold on to a tulip," panted Flynn.

He and Elmo did so, and they rapidly disappeared downwards with the flowers.

In the tunnel below, the Mechanical Digger was eating away at the earth, with Sinapse, singing happily, at the controls. Unseen by the dotty inventor, Flynn crept forward and tried to attach his magnet to the body of the chomping machine. He almost made it, but at the final moment he dropped the magnet. Worse still, it fell between

the vicious tracks of the Digger – right out of his reach!

Now it was Elmo's turn to be a hero. He buzzed into action beneath the Digger's underbelly and retrieved the magnet. Flynn thanked his brave pal, then made another attempt to affix the magnet onto the machine. This time it worked!

"A-ha!" cackled Sinapse, rejoicing in the destruction he was bringing. "With one of these little beauties, they could have built the Channel Tunnel years ago!"

He failed to notice the compass needle, affected by the magnet's field, flip round from north to south. But then he glanced down at the instrument to check his position. "Hey, I'm going completely in the wrong direction! How did that happen? Never mind...left hand down a bit and full steam ahead for Flower City!"

As Sinapse and his Digger bumbled off, *away* from the City, Flynn turned his attention to a group of worker Kruds slavishly cutting up the stolen tulips for firewood. Wasabi was in charge, so working conditions were far from pleasant!

Flynn stole past the Kruds and reached a neat log-delivery machine parked farther down the tunnel. Fugg was in the driver's seat – and fast asleep! With a wicked smirk, Flynn pulled a flare from his bag and placed it in the machine's little tender. The flare went off like a brilliant firework, gushing out coloured smoke. Fugg woke with a start and his knee hit the 'forward' lever. His machine immediately shot at full speed down the tunnel. It

zoomed past the workers and then, with an almighty bang, smashed into the wayward Digger!

Up above, the Verigreens cheered. They watched the tulips stop disappearing and heard the bang that signalled the end of the Digger.

"He's done it!" shouted Godfrey. "Amazing!" beamed Alex.

In the Stump, Draffsack was gloating about the victory over the Verigreens that he believed was taking place. "As we speak, your Majesty, our dark and powerful machine is tugging at the roots of Flower City. Swarms of Verries will be running around – oh, no!"

He'd been rudely interrupted by the unexpected arrival of the mangled Digger – through the floor in front of him! Sinapse jumped down, all coloured and foolish. "All change for Great Yarmouth! Mind the gap! Ding, ding!" he chortled.

Then Wasabi and Fugg appeared. Yes, you guessed it – they were brightly coloured and almost helpless with laughter too!

"You brainless, witless oafs," began Draffsack. That was all he had time to say, for the Queen was not amused and she had plans for him. "Draffsack, you and I need to have a little chat. Follow me...!"

"I'm a dead man," said Draffsack simply.

How much does Fugg get a week? **A tenner!**

Max: Mummy, Mummy, I don't want to go abroad... **Katheter:** Shut up and start swimming!

Why do Kruds wear black braces with brown spots? **To keep their trousers up!**

Knock, knock! Who's there? **Fugg!** Fugg who? **Fugg-et the jokes and let me in!**

How do we know Katheter should have studied harder? **She hasn't enough degrees!**

Why is six scared of seven? **Because seven ate nine!**

Why would Fagin make a good Krud? **He's got pinchers!**

How do the Methane Brothers cut a cake? **In sectors!**

Why is the Thorn Swamp a good place to find a bank? **There are branches everywhere!**

Which way do sardines point? **With their fish fingers!**

Groan with the Kruds

What is Wasabi's favourite chat-up line? **I gotta crush on you!**

Drumsturdy: What's the difference between a buffalo and a bison? **Greeb:** You can't wash your hands in a buffalo!

Why does Sinapse keep losing his glasses? **He's got no ears!**

Why does Katheter do the Lottery? **"It Krud be you...!"**

What piece of jewellery does Katheter need most? **A charm bracelet!**

What's a Krud's favourite swimming stroke? **The crawl!**

Peg's puzzles

Answers on Page 61

COLOUR CODE

In Peg's alphabet, each vowel (A, E, I, O and U) has been replaced by a colour. What does this message say?

Y██ █ND █ █R█ M██T█NG GR██B █ND█R TH█ GR██T FL█W█R █N M█ND█Y █T █L█V█N

CHANGE THE WORD

Can you change CAT to DOG in three moves, altering just one letter at a time but still making a word? When you've done that, try changing TEA to POT...

CAT	TEA
___	___
___	___
DOG	POT

BRICKS IN THE WALL

Oh dear, Peg has demolished a wall in Krud City. How many bricks (all the same size) will they need to repair it?

SPOT THE DIFFERENCE

There are six differences between these two pictures. Can you find them all?

54

JUMBLIES

Whoops, Peg's spelling is not his strong point! Can you re-arrange these Insektor words?

EXAL	FERYDOG
KNOTSIRE	PULIT
WOLFER	SUKIPOO

SHARING OUT THE SWEETS

It's Elmo's birthday and he has a bag of sweets. He gives Peg a quarter of them, and shares the rest equally between himself, Alex and Max. If Max gets 3 sweets, how many did Elmo have to begin with?

ELMO'S MINI QUIZ

1. **How man different types of insects are there?**
   (a) 100 (b) 1,000 (c) 1,000,000

2. **Boy, can fleas *jump*! But how high?**
   (a) Five times their own body length
   (b) Ten times
   (c) A hundred times

3. **For how many years have insects been around?**
   (a) A million
   (b) 45 million   (c) 370 million

4. **For each person on Earth, how many insects are there?**
   (a) 50,000   (b) 1,000,000
   (c) 100,000,000

WHICH WAY?

The Verries have found Sinapse's new crane – very complicated, as usual! Which way must they turn the handle to raise the bundle of flower wood?

FRUIT & FLOWERS

Fill in these words correctly and you'll find the name of one of your favourite characters reading downwards in the yellow squares!

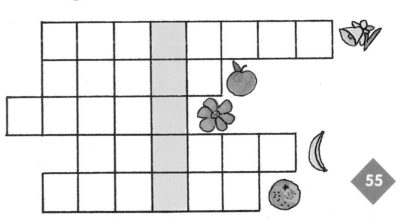

Flynn was on Krud patrol. In other words, he was spending a leisurely afternoon flying around the skies with Peg!

"It's quiet, Peg...too quiet," said Flynn, like cowboys do just before the baddies gallop into town and wreck the place. "Let's head east and look for Kruds. They're bound to be up to something..."

It wasn't long before they did spot Krud activity – of sorts. Flynn landed and found it was Max jumping around with excitement.

"I've done it at last!" he chuckled. " I've actually managed to dig a tunnel that's got me out of the City!"

"Does your mummy know you're out?" Flynn teased him.

"Oh, no, she's a nightmare! Watches me like a hawk!"

"At least you know who your mother is," sighed Flynn. "I don't know mine, nor my father. Not a clue about either of them."

Peg started honking, but Flynn ignored him and continued chatting to Max. He honked again, then again even louder.

"Alright, Peg...don't overdo it," scolded Flynn.

But then his faithful four-legged friend keeled over and collapsed onto the floor!

"Peg! What's up!?" he cried, rushing to his side.

Godfrey and Alex were walking nearby. They heard Flynn's cry of alarm and they came running. Godfrey bent over Peg and tended to him.

"Do something, Father!" implored Alex.

"Oh, dear, I'm afraid I can't. He's a machine with an organic brain," said Godfrey sorrowfully. "Perhaps I should have told you earlier...Peg is actually an invention of the Kruds."

"The Kruds!" chorused Alex, Flynn and Max.

Godfrey explained that the only way to help Peg was to retrieve his blueprint plans from Krud City. Max suggested the library, the place where Greeb's sandwiches and everything else of importance to the Kruds were stored. But how to get inside?

"Got it!" cried Flynn. "Max's new tunnel! Let's go!"

In the Krud library the place was stuffed with every book ever published in Krud – all as dull as ditchwater and not one joke to be found anywhere!

"Hmm...a hundred ways to capture a Verigreen," murmured Flynn, as he and Max thumbed through volume after boring volume.

Suddenly Sinapse bumbled in. "Single decker buses of the world...would that be under S, D or B?" he mumbled, deep in thought.

Flynn and Max hid quickly but Flynn knocked over a heavy book, which crashed noisily to the floor.

"By heck – it's Verigreens!" shouted Sinapse. "Guards, guards!"

From outside the door, Drumsturdy responded with lightning reflexes. "Och, if I'm not mistaken, that came from the library!"

"That reminds me," said Greeb. "I must take my book back..."

The pair of dopes ran into the library and chased the Verigreens round and round without ever getting near them, whilst Sinapse

looked on and shouted useless advice like, "Get 'em, boys!" At last, Flynn pulled a movable bookshelf across the aisle to block the path of the two guards. But Drumsturdy simply barged into it and sent a multitude of books flying everywhere. Sinapse ended up with a book of single deckers on his nose – and in front of Max landed Peg's plans!

"Flynn!" yelled Max. "We've got it!"

With Flynn reading from the construction manual, Godfrey was soon able to diagnose Peg's complaint. It was a simple enough fault: just a rotten rubber flange behind the main spigot!

"This is all Krud to me," groaned Flynn, studying the blueprint.

"You're useless!" grinned Alex. "Give it here!"

She pulled, and Flynn pulled back. The book ripped apart and a loose page fluttered to the floor. Alex picked it up, and Max looked over her shoulder.

"It's a letter – in Ancient Krud," he said.

"Read it!" said Alex.

"Yeah, go on," added Flynn.

Godfrey was tired of their bickering. He was in acute danger of soldering his finger to Peg's differential. "Just pass me the manual and – um – get lost, will you!"

Alex, Flynn and Max took him at his word. They sat in the Forest, and

Max set to work translating the letter.

"October 25th...sad day again," he began. "Determined my son...should not walk the soulless corridors of Krud City. Have designed robot...to carry him safely to the flowered world. My dearest wish that the Verigreens will welcome my son – ohhh!"

"My son? My son who!?" asked Flynn.

"Hope you like surprises, 'cos this is a big one!" said Max looking grave. He continued reading: "My dearest wish that the Verigreens will welcome my son, Flynn."

The three of them were still staring in shocked silence at one another when Godfrey arrived with Peg. He was now well and honking madly! Godfrey was surprised by the lack of attention he received.

It was Flynn who spoke first. "Is there anything you want to tell me?"

"Well, I don't know..." said Godfrey, mystified.

"Peg brought Flynn here, didn't he!?" blurted out Alex.

"I'm just a Krud!" cried Flynn.

Godfrey's eyes misted over. "I should apologise, Flynn...I've kept this secret from you for far too long. But now I must tell you exactly what happened...

"Several years ago I was walking in the Daffodil Plantation, when I came across Peg with a tiny baby. It was you, Flynn, and you were a very attractive young fellow – then! Over

your head floated a mystical sphere which issued a personal message from your father, who appears to have been a great scientist and philosopher."

"Wow!" exclaimed Max.

Godfrey continued. "'I am Magus, chief scientific advisor to Queen Katheter,' said the sphere. 'Because of my peaceful beliefs, I will soon be arrested and imprisoned – my fate uncertain. I entrust my son Flynn to the care of the Verigreens, to be loved as one of your own. Hopefully our two nations will one day enjoy peace and I shall be re-united with my son...'"

"He sounds an amazing guy!" exclaimed Alex.

"But where is he? Is he still alive?" demanded Flynn.

"I just don't know," replied Godfrey. "Anyway, I bathed you daily in the Energy Pool and you became one of the family. It was such a happy day when I held you up to baby Alex and told her to say hello to her new brother!"

Flynn said nothing. He jumped onto Peg – now fully airworthy again – and took to the skies.

"Where are you going!?" shouted Godfrey.

"To think. I need to think," came the reply.

Alex looked fed up. "I wish I'd never found that wretched piece of paper. It's all my fault."

"No, he had to find out sometime," Godfrey consoled her. "There's never a right time for news like this..."

Flynn and Peg flew over the water towards the Stump. He didn't know whether he was angry and bitter or just upset. "You and me, Peg...both Kruds! I don't believe it. I hate Kruds."

Peg honked sympathetically.

"Thanks – I knew you were on my side," said Flynn. "Whoops! Hey, what are you doing?"

Peg had decided to cheer up the young Verigreen. He turned into helicopter mode and began doing breathtaking mid-air rolls, honking with delight. It worked! The exhilarating ride made Flynn feel much better.

"I'm so grateful to Godfrey for looking after me," he said. "Krud, Verigreen...I know it doesn't really matter. I'm just not used to it yet. Come on, Peg. We're going home!"

With that, Peg and Flynn turned right round in the blue sky and headed back to the Great Flower.

GOODBYE-EE!

Well, that's it for now...hope you've had lots of Insektor fun! And next time you see an insect, remember to be kind – or you may find a dreaded Krudmobile on your tail! Have a great New Year ...and see you again soon!

The Verigreens and The Kruds

ANSWERS

Page II

Page 23

Page 24

SPOT THE DIFFERENCE

Page 46
FAMILY TREE

I Prism
2 Godfrey
3 Alex   4 Flynn
5 Bentley   6 Peg   7 Elmo

FAMILY TANGLE

I Katheter
4 Max
2 Draffsach 3 Fugg 5 Kopious 6 Sinapse
7 Drumsturdy 8 Greeb 9 Wasabi 10 Methane Brothers

JUMBLIES
ALEX, GODFREY, INSEKTOR, TULIP, FLOWER, KOPIOUS

Pages 54 and 55

COLOUR CODE
YOU AND I ARE MEETING GREEB UNDER THE GREAT FLOWER ON MONDAY AT ELEVEN

CHANGE THE WORD
CAT	TEA
COT	PEA
COG	PET
DOG	POT

BRICKS IN THE WALL
Thirty four bricks are needed

SHARING OUT THE SWEETS
Twelve sweets

ELMO'S MINI QUIZ
1. All correct answers are (c)!

WHICH WAY?
Anti-clockwise

FRUIT AND FLOWERS

```
D A F  F  O D  I L
A P P  L  E
D A I  S  Y
    B A N  A N A
  O R A N  G E
```